Samuel Sharpe

The Triple Mummy Case of Aroeri-Ao, an Egyptian Priest

SALZWASSER
VERLAG

Samuel Sharpe

The Triple Mummy Case of Aroeri-Ao, an Egyptian Priest

Reprint of the original.

1st Edition 2023　|　ISBN: 978-3-37514-756-3

Verlag (Publisher): Salzwasser Verlag GmbH, Zeilweg 44, 60439 Frankfurt, Deutschland
Vertretungsberechtigt (Authorized to represent): E. Roepke, Zeilweg 44, 60439 Frankfurt, Deutschland
Druck (Print): Books on Demand GmbH, In de Tarpen 42, 22848 Norderstedt, Deutschland

THE TRIPLE MUMMY CASE

OF

AROERI - AO

AN EGYPTIAN PRIEST,

IN DR. LEE'S MUSEUM AT HARTWELL HOUSE,

BUCKINGHAMSHIRE.

DRAWN BY JOSEPH BONOMI

AND DESCRIBED BY SAMUEL SHARPE:

PUBLISHED FOR

THE SYRO-EGYPTIAN SOCIETY OF LONDON.

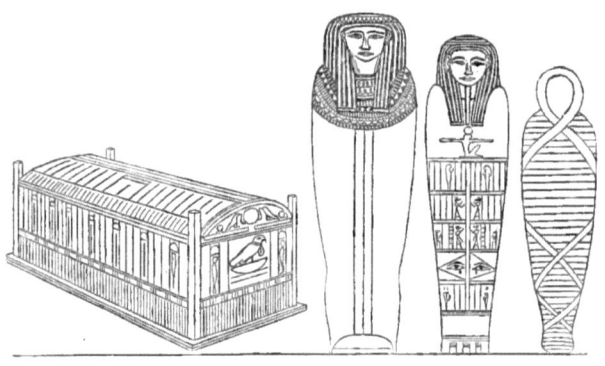

LONDON:

LONGMAN, BROWN, GREEN, LONGMANS, AND ROBERTS.

1858.

THE TRIPLE MUMMY CASE OF AROERI-AO.

THIS valuable case, or rather cases, with the mummy which they once held, were sent to England by Mr. Salt, the British Consul-General in Egypt, and were then sold to Mr. Pettigrew, the well-known writer on mummies, and by him again to Dr. Lee. They are, first, an outer case with four straight sides and an arched top; secondly, a middle case, shaped to the body, with a carved head and face; and thirdly, an inner case, also shaped to the body, with carved head and face. Within the innermost once lay the embalmed body wrapped in linen bandages. These Mr. Pettigrew unrolled in the lecture room of the Royal Institution, before a large audience; and an account of the appearance of the mummy on being thus opened was published in the *Morning Chronicle* for May 30th, 1836. Mr. Pettigrew then read the name of the embalmed man as Asiriao.

The linen bandages were several hundred yards in length, and beneath them were four large linen sheets. The viscera had been removed and rolled up, and placed between the legs : the liver had been placed in the abdomen. The head was completely shaven, as was usual with Egyptian priests. The body was that of an aged man ; and some parts of it had been gilt, a circumstance which is not surprising when we consider the costly style of the three cases. It thus appears that the embalmed man was an aged priest, belonging to a wealthy family.

It was at one time thought that the bandages of the Egyptian mummies were of cotton cloth, from a doubt about the meaning of the words used by Herodotus ; and even experienced eyes were unable to determine whether they were of linen or cotton, in consequence of their stained condition. But lately the microscope has enabled us to distinguish between the smooth natural fibre of the cotton and the irregular ragged fibre of the linen. I believe that wherever careful examination has been made the bandages are found to be linen. Linen cloth had, from the earliest times, been manufactured in Egypt. It was not till after the trade had been opened with India that cotton was known in the valley of the Nile.

The sides of the cases are held together by rude mortised joints, which are made fast by wooden pegs. The outer case has at each corner a small upright square post to which the sides are fixed. This rises as high as the arch of the top. But the carpenter's work is not exact, and the spaces between the planks, when they do not fit, are filled up with plaster made of earth and gum. In some mummy cases the wood-work is in part held together by cloth bandages; but no such fastenings appear to have been used here.

The value of the wood is curiously shown by the care which the maker has taken to save it. First, because by measurement we find that the cases are thinner than they seem to be, as judged by the thickness of the edges shown. The edges of the middle case are two inches thick, but the top and bottom of each case, where the thickness is not seen, are only seven-eighths of an inch thick. This is shown in fig. 3, Plate 1. And secondly, because the planks out of which they are made, though of an even thickness, are not of an even width; they had not been previously cut down so as to have their edges made straight. We see that unnecessary waste of wood was avoided, by our finding the bottom of the outer case made of such pieces as have the unevenness of one fitted into the unevenness of the other. This is shown in fig. 2, Plate 1.

The square outer case is of sycamore wood. The middle case is of cedar. The face on the middle case is of dark acacia wood, with eyelids and eyebrows of dark bronze, and eyes of ivory. The inner case, like the outer, is probably of sycamore. The pegs are of acacia wood. The paint with which the cases are covered is a water-colour made of gum from the acacia tree. The colours are six in number :　The white is of powdered limestone ;

　　　　　The red and yellow are ochres ;

　　　　　The blue and green are of copper ;

　　　　　The black is of charcoal.

These are the usual materials of the Egyptian paints. The last five are all laid upon a thick surface of white, and are varnished with an ancient varnish of resin, or perhaps amber, dissolved in spirit. But the white paint is left free from varnish, in order that it should not lose its whiteness when the varnish changes its colour. But the cases are none of them free from touches of modern paint and modern varnish, which, however, in no instances, seem to have obscured or falsified the hieroglyphics. The whole is in excellent condition.

Of the materials above spoken of, the acacia and sycamore trees grow in Egypt, but the greater number are foreign. The cedar may have been brought from the island of Cyprus, or from Tyre at the foot of Mount Lebanon, or from Tarsus at the foot of Mount Taurus; from all of which places Egypt supplied its own want of timber. The bronze and copper were from Cyprus, an island rich in copper mines, and which gave its name to that metal; or from the mines in the range of Mount Sinai, which were worked even before the time of Moses. No copper is found in Egypt. The ivory of which the eyes are made was brought to Egypt both down the Nile from Ethiopia and by the traders on the Red Sea. The amber, of which the varnish was probably made, was found abundantly on the shores of the Red Sea. It seems to be represented among the tributes to Thothmosis III., in his great procession, in the form of large beads strung upon a string. It was cut into ornaments for the Egyptian ladies, and perhaps received its Greek name, *berenice*, from one of the Egyptian queens; and we thence have the German name *bernstein*; and, according to a happy conjecture, the Latin and English words *vernix, varnish*, and the Roman Catholic saint *Veronica*, the patroness of the painters.

It was not unusual in the Egyptian mummies to have a portrait of the deceased person painted on the cloth which was laid upon the face; and one of these mummy-cloths, with a portrait on it, may have given rise to the story that Saint Veronica was one of the women who followed the Saviour to the cross, and wiped his face with her handkerchief, and then found his portrait miraculously impressed upon it.

Figure 2, in Plate 1, is a view of the bandaged mummy lying in its three cases, of which two are shaped to the body, and one is made with straight sides. The lid of each case has been lifted off.

Figure 3 is a section of the same, showing the proportion between the body, the bandages, and the three cases. The outer case is seven feet three inches long.

The Top of the Outer Case.

On the arched top of the outer case, Plate 1, figure 1, is a single line of hieroglyphics between two rows of pictures and writing. The pictures are ten in number. Four of these contain, each, a hawk bandaged as a mummy, sitting on a dish, with an eye and dish written over it as its name. On the head of each is a flame or glory. From other monuments we may glean that this bird represents the soul of the deceased, and the two characters for its name may be so read as to give us that meaning. The eye is ⲃⲁⲗ, and the dish is NIB; and the two may perhaps be read as ⲃⲱⲗ ⲛⲓⲃⲉ, *the released breath*. But they more probably mean Baal Nebo. And observing, as we often may, that the Babylonians and Assyrians, like the Greeks and Romans afterwards, were ever fond of borrowing their superstitions from Egypt, we may reasonably suppose that the Babylonian gods Baal and Nebo had both Egyptian names, from BAL, *the eye* of Providence, and NEBO, *Lord*.

Four other pictures contain, each, a figure of the deceased priest, with a glory on his shaven head, his skin red in colour, and a white tunic hanging from his waist to his ancles, and upheld by a strap over one shoulder. His hands are raised in the act of prayer to the god Osiris, who stands before him. This god is in the form of a mummy, with a beard, holding a tall Anubis-staff in his hands, and wearing the crown of Upper Egypt. Behind each Osiris stands another god, with a glory on his head, and holding in his hands an ostrich feather, the usual emblem of truth. These four gods are the four lesser gods of the dead. They should have four different heads, namely, a man's, a jackal's, an ape's, and a hawk's. Amset *the carpenter*, with a man's head; Hepe *the digger*, with an ape's head; Snouf *the bleeder*, with a hawk's head; and Smotef or Sottef *the cutter*, with a jackal's head. (See *Egyptian Inscriptions*, plate 16; and Wilkinson's *Materia Hieroglyphica*, I. 50.) But here, by a mistake of the artist, or more probably by a mistake of some modern artist who has rashly undertaken to restore an injured part, two of these gods have human heads, and the jackal's head is wanting. In the inside of the middle case of this mummy, in Plate 4, we see that Smotef there has a hawk's head; and the same is the case in our Plate 6, so probably the same heads did not invariably belong to the same gods.

The two middle pictures are the most important. In one is a boat floating on the water. In it sits the god Horus-Ra, called by the Greeks Aroeris, or the elder Horus, to distinguish him from Horus the son of Isis, when in later times the god Horus became divided into two. Horus-Ra has a hawk's head, with the sun in the place of a crown; and he holds the ostrich feather in his hands. The deceased priest took his name from Horus-Ra, and hence this god naturally holds the first place on the mummy case. Above him, like a canopy, is a sacred snake, the Uræus, wearing the crown of Upper Egypt. This is painted blue like the canopy of heaven. Behind Horus-Ra stands Horus the son of Isis, known by his hawk's head, and the double crown of Upper and Lower Egypt. Near him is an eye for his name, from which we learn that he was also called Baal, from ẞᴊλ *an eye*. Horus holds the rudder as steersman of the boat, while it is pushed forward by the deceased man himself, who stands at the prow and holds a long pole, which he thrusts to the bottom of the shallow water which they are crossing. In front of him is written his name, " The deified Aroeri, deceased." Upon the inner case of this mummy we shall see that his name is written at greater length, Aroeri-ao. The ornament at each end of the boat is either a lotus flower or bunch of papyrus flowers.

The other middle picture represents the blue vault of heaven, under the form of a woman, the goddess Neith, whose legs, body, and outstretched arms reach from the ground on one side to the ground on the other. Beneath this vault is the deceased priest, with two bodies. By his death he is divided into two parts. His earthly body is red, and is in the act of falling to the ground. His spiritual or heavenly body is blue, and stands upright, raising his hands to heaven. In this interesting way did the Egyptians express in a picture their belief in the immortality of the soul, or rather their belief that man does not die when his body falls to earth ; making use of the same figure as the Apostle Paul, who says, in 1 Cor. xv. 44, " There is an animal body, and there is a " spiritual body." This picture may be placed in contrast with the older representations of life being put back into the mouth of the mummy, which made the resurrection of the body part of the means necessary to the enjoyment of a future life. In the opinion of this artist the resurrection of the earthly body would seem unnecessary. On each side of this group is a figure of the god Kneph-Ra, seated on a bird's perch. He is known by the ram's head and horns, and by the sun on his head. His name Kneph means *the spirit*, so he naturally forms part of this scene.

Along each side of this top is an ornamental border formed of a row of trees, a border often employed in the Egyptian pictures to mark the boundary of a garden, and sometimes of what seems meant for a heavenly paradise.

The single line of hieroglyphics in the middle of this top may be read (line 1), " A royal gift, dedicated to Anubis, the devourer of what is given to the mummy, holy in the temples of the land of Sais, of the land of Amenti, and of the city of Hermonthis, for the prayers of the deified Aroeri, a man deceased, son of the priest Soten-Vaphra deceased, son of the priest Onk-Chonso deceased, son of the priest Horseisi deceased, blessed."

The reasons for so translating these characters may be given as follows, and they will explain how far certainty has been reached in the art of decyphering a line of hieroglyphics, of which this is one of the easiest, from the recurrence of well-known words. It will not be necessary to explain the rest of the hieroglyphics on these cases so minutely.

The twig, No. 1, is SO, from ℧o, *a plant.* It is the name of one of the four chief orders of priests ; and when it has the addition of an insect, which is the name of a second of those orders, it forms the title of the king. Hence it may be here translated *royal,* or perhaps *priestly.*

The pyramid, No. 2, is ⲧⲁⲧ, *a hill,* and hence readily used for ⲧⲏⲓ, *a gift.* This character is the original of the Greek letter Δ, and is a T in the name Domitianus. We may digress to say that another name for the pyramid is ⲡⲁⲱⲱ, *a mountain,* or with the article, ⲛⲓⲡⲁⲱⲱ, *the mountain* ; and hence its well-known name *pyramid.*

The next three characters are OTP, from ⲱⲧⲉⲃ, *to consecrate,* or *dedicate.* They also form the last half of the name of king Amun-othph, which Eratosthenes translates *dedicated to Amun.* Thus the meaning of these characters, which we gain from the Coptic language, is confirmed by the remark of Eratosthenes.

The horizontal stroke, No. 6, is the modern and slovenly way of writing the N, used in place of the wavy line for which it stands. The wavy line is used on the two inner cases, which are more carefully painted than this. It is the preposition ⲛⲁ, *unto.* This is the original of the Hebrew letter ב. The position of the letter is changed, but the shape is the same. This change of position is common when one alphabet is formed from another.

The next three letters, No. 7, 8, 9, are ANP, Anubis, the dog-headed or jackal-headed god.

Of the next four characters, the first three, No. 10, 11, 12, are KOT; and if the fourth, No. 13, is B or F, the whole may be the word ⲕⲱⲧⲉⲃ, or ⲭⲟⲧϥ, *to wound, to tear, to carry off.* The first character is the original of the Greek letter X, which was originally written thus, +. Hence I venture to translate this group as *devourer.* The less known fourth character is a bag, and may be ϩⲱⲃ, *a skin.*

The arm and hand holding a pyramid, No. 14, is the verb *to give,* being the same in sound as the pyramid itself, which we have explained as the noun *a gift.* The arm is in the act of presenting the gift. The horned snake which follows it is the Coptic suffix ϥ, or F. It changes the verb into a noun or past participle; and the two together are *what is given*. This latter character is the original of the Hebrew, Coptic, and Greek letters ٦, ϥ, and F, much as they now seem to differ. The last reached Greece through the Phenicians of the island of Cyprus.

The next four characters mean *the mummy case*, and are explained by that which follows, which is a view of the end of this very mummy case, and is added as a demonstrative sign. The first two are K R, and represent the word ⲭⲁⲣⲱ, *silent*, from which was derived the name of Charon, whose employment was to ferry the dead over the river Styx. The second two are sometimes the word *sculptor*, or *carver*, as known from pictures where he is employed on his work. And thus we are led by the demonstrative sign to understand two groups, which elsewhere certainly mean *silent* and *carver*, as here meaning *the carved box for the dead body*, or *the mummy case*. We have many other instances of the demonstrative sign being required to distinguish between the person and the thing. And this explains that it is only in the case of the demonstrative sign that hieroglyphics are picture writing; in all other cases they are true writing. In pictures there is no resemblance between a libation and a priest, between a sacrifice and a sacrificer; but in our written English they only differ by one letter. And so it is in hieroglyphics.

The three characters, No. 21, 22, and 23, are B F R, and may perhaps be pronounced Vaphra, which was the name of one of the kings, though he did not write his name with these letters. The first, when alone, is the word ⲟⲩⲁⲃ, *holy*, *good*, and has the force of B, F, or V; and, with the others added, it has still the same meaning as when alone. It is the letter B in the name of Labaris, and in ⲛⲟⲩⲏⲃ, *a priest*; it is PH in Mesaphra and Scemiophra, and in other less certain names. Indeed the right reading of the name of queen Scemiophra is of first importance in Egyptian chronology. She is the immediate predecessor of king Amasis on the tablet of Abydos; and

Scemiophra. thus the tablet proves that Manetho's XIIth dynasty is immediately followed by his XVIIIth.

The full-faced owl, No. 24, and again, No. 26, is an M or MO, from ⲙⲁⲁⲩ, *an owl*, known in the compound word ⲕⲁⲕⲕⲁⲙⲁⲁⲩ, *the night owl*. It is here the preposition *in*, from ⲙⲁ, *a place*.

No. 25 is the picture of a building. The mallet, or hatchet, like a flag on the top, is the character for *God*, so used from the resemblance of the two words ⲛⲟⲩⲧⲉ, *God*, and ⲛⲟⲩⲧ, *to bruise*. It makes the building into *a temple*, or *house of God*.

No. 27 to 30 are STT-*land*. The last is the demonstrative sign; and I venture to think the letters mean *Sais*, though that city is usually spelt SS.

No. 31 to 34 are the name of Amenti, which is the region of the dead, or, when it means a spot upon earth, as probably here, it is a district of Thebes, on the west side of the river. The first character is formed of M and T united; the feather is M, used for Amun; and the perch on which it stands is T.

No. 35 to 37 are the name of a city ending with the demonstrative sign for *city*; and I agree with Mr. Harris, in his *Hieroglyphical Standards*, in thinking that it is Hermonthis. The circular picture of a city has the sound of ⲕⲁⲉⲓ, and also of the letter K; and hence, by a confusion of the sounds K and TH, arising from the use of the guttural which is intermediate between the two, it became the original of the Greek Θ, which at first had the form of this character.

No. 38, the horizontal line, is the letter N, the preposition *for*.

No. 39 is a pair of arms held up in the act of prayer. It is a K, from ⲭϭⲟⲓ, *an arm*. No. 40 is the vowel E or I. Together they form the word *prayer* or *adoration*, or *sacred offering*. The K is the original of the Hebrew ⲃ, changed in position, as already remarked. The I is the original of the Greek I and Hebrew ⲓ.

No. 41, 42, and 43 are the oft-recurring name of the god Osiris. Of these the last is the word *god*; the throne is *Isi*, and the eye is *ro*, making *Isi-ro, god*. Pictorial reasons seem to have guided the priests in writing this word. The eye is in all other cases a vowel; and here we should expect to find the mouth used for RO, but in this important word the mouth has been changed into an eye, as if it were the all-seeing eye of Providence; and it has been placed as the first character instead of the last. Again, it was one of their religious opinions that every good man, on his death, took upon himself the nature of Osiris; and the mummies are often ornamented with the sceptres of that god; hence this group is used as an adjective for *deified*, and, as such, applied to the deceased man in this place.

The following four characters, No. 44, 45, 46, and 47, are the man's name. The feather is A. The sitting figure, putting his hand to his mouth, is RO, from po, *a mouth*; or, if he is putting his hand to his head, is ⲉⲣⲣⲟ, *a king*, or *priest wearing a crown*. This last is better drawn on the Rosetta stone, and there could not be mistaken for the baby not yet able to talk, which here it too much resembles. This latter has his legs hanging down, as in figure 13, and is an S, from the Coptic ϣⲏⲣⲓ, *a son*. The mouth is R, from po, *a mouth*. But as it is followed by a vowel, the syllabic sound which attaches to it probably precedes it, and it may be ER. The stroke is the vowel I. Together they make the name Aroeri. Its sound is confirmed by our finding, in figure 19, line 4, the name spelt with a mouth for R, in place of the sitting figure.

No. 48 is the demonstrative sign, the sitting figure of a man. In the case of a king this sign is not used, because the oval ring which incloses his name answers the same purpose. In some other cases the word ⲡⲁⲛϥ, *his name*, is written in hieroglyphics before the name, either with or without this sitting figure after it.

No. 49 and 50 are the word MO, *deceased*, from ⲙⲟⲩ, *death*. Among the various forms of the letters M and O, these two are the forms usually chosen to spell this word.

No. 51 and 52, SE, *son*. The goose is S, from ϭⲉⲩⲉ, *a goose*.

No. 53 and 54 is *priest*, being the word ⲛⲟⲩⲧⲉ, *god*.

No. 55 to 59, Soten-Vaphra, the name of the deceased man's father. The rabbit is SOT, from ϭⲱⲧϩ, *to burrow*. And it is so named in the paintings when its hieroglyphical name is written over it. The horizontal line is N. Together they form the word ⲥⲟⲧⲱⲛ, *righteous*; and on the Rosetta stone it bears an analogous meaning several times, as *lawful, appointed, decreed*. The words *Soten-Vaphra*, which are here a proper name, are, as *righteous and holy*, often applied to the god Osiris (as in line 20), and often in praise to men when dead.

No. 60 and 61 are as before, MO, *deceased*.

No. 62 and 63 are as before, SE, *son*.

No. 64 and 65 are as before, ⲛⲟⲩⲧⲉ, *a priest*.

No. 66 to 69 are Onk-Chonso, a man's name. The first character, sometimes called the *crux ansata*, is ⲱⲛϩ, *life*, whether written alone, as here, or with two more letters, NK. The latter characters are the name of the Theban god Chonso, who is usually a boy with his finger to his mouth, and wearing a single lock of hair. He plays the same part in the Theban trinity, with his parents Amun-Ra and Athor, as Horus in the Memphite trinity, with Osiris and Isis.

No. 70 and 71 are as before, MO, *deceased*.

No. 72 and 73 are as before, SE, *son*.

No. 74 and 75 are as before, ⲛⲟⲧⲧⲉ, *priest*.

No. 76 to 81 arc Hor-se-isi, a man's name, which may be translated *Horus the son of Isis*. The hawk is Horus. The throne is Isis, from ⲍ̣ⲉⲥⲓ, *to sit*, perhaps pronounced Hesi. It is in the older and more carefully written inscriptions followed by TS, the feminine termination, from the suffix ⲧⲥ, *her*; here it is in a less usual manner followed by TT.

No. 82 and 83 are as before, MO, *deceased*.

No. 84 to 86 is a group which often ends a sentence, either as an adjective of praise, or as an ejaculation of blessing. The feather is A. The circle is K, as it is usually marked with cross bars, which distinguish it from an R. The middle character is doubtful; it may be an instrument for bathers to scrape themselves with, and bear the sound of OK, from ⲍ̣ⲱⲕ, *to scrape*. As such it seems to be the first syllable in the name of the Memphite king Uchora. The group may mean *made into a mummy*, from ⳉⲟⲕ, *to bandage*. But its exact meaning is doubtful.

The other hieroglyphics of figure 1 may be read as follows: (line 2) " Honour to the deified (3) Aroeri deceased, son of the priest (4) Soten-Vaphra deceased, son (5) of the priest Onk-Chonso deceased, son (6) of the priest Hor-se-isi deceased. (7) His mother is the lady Moutresi (8) deceased."

The meaning of the following five lines is not so clear; but we may remark that line 10 begins with the name of Thebes, spelt APE, and followed by a circle, the demonstrative sign for a city. If before these letters we place the feminine article T, we have TAPE, *the chief city*, or *Thebes*. In line 13 the word Osiris, meaning *deified*, is spelt with another form of S, far more common than the throne which, though usually the second character in this word, is not met with in many other words. The throne, as a character for S, is almost peculiar to the words Isis and Osiris.

The other hieroglyphics on the lid are, (line 15) " A royal gift, dedicated to Horus-Ra, (16) D. s., chief of the heavenly gods; Chem, (17) lord of the city of San; Pthah-Sokar-(18)-Osiris, chief of * * temple; (19) Anubis * * god, lord of Ethiopia; (20) Osiris, the good judge. (21) Offerings of things dedicated, things sacred, (22) other good libations, D. s., (23) other * * for the prayers of the deified (24) Aroeri deceased, son of the priest (25) Soten-Vaphra deceased, blessed." (Line 14) " Blessed by Osiris," or embalmed and deified.

The figure of the hawk, for Horus, follows directly his name Horus-Ra-god (lines 15, 16), and thus the thought is written twice, once by means of the letters, and once by the demonstrative sign. We thus see that the force of the letters was too varying to allow them to be read with certainty even by the Egyptians themselves, and the picture or demonstrative sign was added to supply the exactness required. Indeed the frequent use of the demonstrative sign may satisfy us of the essential inexactness of the Egyptian hieroglyphical writing; and it may console us for our not being always able to read them when this useful sign is wanting.

The characters here (line 16), read as Chem, are T, H, *god*; but when written more at length they are T, H, M, *god*, as in figure 19, line 1. The T and H represent the guttural sound, which the Greeks in this word represented by CH. But as this reading of the semicircular T is not in agreement with its usual force, it will be as well to bring forward other cases to support the interchange between K and T, more particularly because on it rests the reading of the name of queen Nitocris, and on that an important point in Egyptian history. First, we have before remarked that the Greek Θ was, in its earliest form, the same as the circular hieroglyphic, the picture of a city, which usually has the force of K. Again, a second mode of writing the name of this god Chem is with a vulture and the semicircle, characters which often mean MT, MAUT, *mother*; but, when used for the god's name, must be read as KM. Again, the word CHEMI, Egyptians, is sometimes spelt with a finger, T, an owl, M, a quail, O, and three strokes for the plural. In this case, to pronounce the word right, we must give to the T the force of K. Again, Herodotus tells us (lib. ii. 69) that the name of the crocodile was χαμψη, and yet we find it written in hieroglyphics with THMS, the first three being the letters of our word Chem (see Young's *Hieroglyphics*, pl. 41, Lk); and the Crocodile lake, near to Heroopolis, is now called the Lake Timsah. Again, four of the Egyptian months seem to have received Hebrew names, as Pachon, from the Hebrew word bethon, *increase*; Payni, from beni, *fruits*; Epiphi, from abib, *corn*; and Mechir, from mether, *rain*; and in two of these we see that TH is interchanged with CH.

But the name which makes the force of this semicircular character important

Mikera Amunmai Nitocris.

is that of the great Theban builder, the queen of Thothmosis II. It is spelt NT-TR. The N is a vase; both the T's are semicircles; the R is the forepart of a lion. Now Eratosthenes tells us of a queen Nitocris, who governed Thebes for her husband; and he translates her name *Athene the Victorious*. The Greek goddess Athene is of course the Egyptian Neith. Victorious is in Coptic ϫⲣⲟ. Hence we have, in Eratosthenes, a queen's name, which should be spelt in hieroglyphics NT-KRO ; and I confidently pronounce that we have it in the sculptured name of the wife of Thothmosis II., which we should read NT-TR, if the above quoted cases did not authorize us to consider the TH and K or CH as sometimes interchangeable. This is an important point in our Egyptian inquiries, because the historian Manetho adds that Nitocris was the builder of the third pyramid, and the last of the line of Memphite sovereigns; and thus, through the right understanding of this guttural semicircle—usually T, but sometimes K—we are able to prove the marriage of a Memphite queen with a Theban king, and thereby to fix the date when the former lived. We thus shorten the time occupied by Egyptian history, by showing that a race of kings reigned in each of these cities at the same time, down to the marriage of Nitocris with Thothmosis II.

The god Pthah-Sokar-Osiris (lines 17, 18) either received his name from the hill of Saccara, near Memphis, or gave it to that hill. Osiris was at Memphis divided into two characters; this god was one, and the other was Osiris-Apis or Serapis. The latter was worshipped on the hill of Sinope, near Memphis, and hence called the Sinopic Osiris. From this arose an opinion in the time of the Ptolemies that he came from Sinope in Pontus.

Anubis being, in line 19, as often elsewhere, called lord of Ethiopia, leads us to conjecture that he may have received his name from Nubia, which name was itself given to a part of Ethiopia, from ноⲧⲃ, *gold*, which was there found in large quantities in the time of Egypt's prosperity.

Line 22 begins with KT, from ⲭⲉⲧ, *other* ; and the dish, which often means ⲛⲏⲃ, *lord*, and to which we have above given the meaning of ⲛⲃⲉ, *breath*, here must be read as ⲛⲃⲉⲛ, *all*, and simply gives a plural force to the word which it follows. The line ends with three strokes representing waves, which are here the demonstrative sign for *water*. The character before these waves is a leg, on which rests a vase with water flowing from it, a character which would mean priest, unless the waves told us that it meant not the priest himself but the libation which he pours out.

Line 14 begins with the letters AS, the Coptic prefix to a past participle; and it makes the word which may mean " blessing" into " blessed."

The First Side of the Outer Case.

The painting on one side of the square outer case, figure 4, Plate 2, contains seven figures, each in form of a mummy, with a flame or glory on his head, and twenty-two lines of hieroglyphics, which may be translated as follows :

(Line 1) " A royal gift dedicated to Horus-Ra, D. s., chief (2) of the heavenly gods ; Chem, god, lord of San ; Pthah-(3)-Sokar-Osiris * * * * ; (4) Anubis * * god, lord of Ethiopia ; Osiris (5) the righteous good king immortal ; offer-(6) ings of olive oil, thousands of oxen, thousands (7) of geese, thousands of priestly things, (8) thousands of various kinds of money, thousands of (9) other good libations, thousands (10) of other * * * for the deified blessed (11) Aroeri deceased, son of the priest of Amun Sot-(12)-en-Vaphra, deceased ; son of the priest of Amun (13) Onk-Chonso, deceased ; son of the priest of Amun (14) Horseisi, deceased ; son of the priest of (15) Amun * * * * * * * deceased. His mother (16) the lady of the house Hatresi, deceased. The guardian chief (17) lord Osiris, ruler of Amenti, (18) god, chief of Thebes ; gifts of a multi- tude of (19) things dedicated to the land of Amenti. Righteous (20) * * * * (21) * unto the deified Aroeri, deceased, (22) son of the priest of Amun Soten- Vaphra."

In this inscription it will be observed that the order of the lines, and the order of the letters, and also the faces of the letters, are changed. We read from left to right, not as before, in Plate 1, from right to left. In each case, however, the reader meets the faces of the animals, and, as we may describe it, the points of the letters. On the other hand, the Latin, Greek, and Hebrew writing, though not alike as to the order of the letters, yet all agree in making us not meet the points of the letters, but follow their round backs. As examples, take the Latin letters C L E F G, the Greek letters Γ K Σ, and the Hebrew letters ר נ מ כ ד ב. In our own written characters, however, we very much return to the Egyptian custom, and quit that of the Roman alphabet, which we use in printing. We form many of our written letters so that the reader meets the points, as in *B F J P S*.

The word in line 2, read as San, the Egyptian name for the city of Tanis, was illegible in line 17, Plate 1. The first character is a tower, and has the force of S, perhaps from ꟺꟺ *lofty*. It only occurs in this and one other group, which is one name of the goddess Isis.

In line 6 the word *thousands* is ☉o, a lotus leaf, with the force of S; hence ⳩ﻼ, *a thousand*.

In line 8 the word *various kinds* is formed of ϫϵⲧ, *other*, with the letters MN, which, like the prefix ⲙⲛⲧ, make it into a noun substantive.

The mother's name Hatresi, in line 16, may be translated *Heart of her Son*. In figure 1, line 7, it was Moutresi, or *Mother of her Son*.

In line 15 we have another name added to the pedigree of the deceased, in the person of his great great grandfather, in which name however the character of the flying bird is of doubtful sound.

In line 17 the word Amenti is very unnecessarily followed by two demonstrative signs, one the figure of three hills for *country*, and the other a circular *city*. This is a mistake of the artist.

In line 18, the letters O, SH, are translated *multitude*, from ⲱϣ, *many*.

In line 21, the word *deceased* is followed by a T, which makes it into the feminine. This is a mistake, as the deceased person is a man. The same mistake occurs in line 22, and in figure 5, line 18.

The Second Side of the Outer Case.

The second side of the square case, figure 5, Plate 2, contains, like the former, seven standing figures and twenty-two lines of hieroglyphics, as follows :

(Line 1) " Honour to the deified priest of Amun, (2) Aroeri, deceased ; son of the priest of Amun Soten-(3)-Vaphra, D. S., deceased ; son of the priest of Amun Onk-Chonso, (4) deceased ; son of * * * Horseisi, deceased. (5) His mother the lady of the house Moutresi, D. S., deceased. (6) The guardian chief lord Osiris, ruler of Amenti, (7) god, lord of Thebes. Gifts with a multitude of dedications, (8) to Pet-amenti, the good * * * * * (9) * * * * the deified priest (10) of Amun, Aroeri, deceased ; son of the priest of Amun (11) Soten-Vaphra, deceased ; son of * * * Horse-(12)-isi, deceased. His mother the lady of the house Hatresi, (13) D. S., deceased. * de-(18)-ified priest of Amun, Aroeri, deceased ; (19) son of the priest of Amun Soten-Vaphra, D. S., deceased ; (20) son of the priest of Amun Horseisi, deceased. (21) His mother the lady of the house Hatresi, D. S., deceased, (22) blessed by Sokar-Osiris."

Part of this inscription, between lines 13 and 18, is not so easily read. In lines 3 and 19, for the name Vaphra we have only its first letter. In lines 5 and

21, the demonstrative sign which follows the name of the mother is known to be a woman, by the lotus flower which she holds in her hands, and also by her two knees being together as she sits upon her heels, instead of having one knee raised, as it is in the figures of the men. In line 5 the adjective which follows is in the feminine gender, having the feminine article T placed between the two letters M and O, of the word deceased. In the Coptic language of the second century of the Christian era this article is always prefixed: in the hieroglyphics it is more usually postfixed, though sometimes, as in this word, it is inserted before the last letter. In line 8, Pet-Amenti, the title of Osiris, is formed like the Egyptian name Potiphar in Genesis xxxix., and Potipherah in Genesis xli.; the first means belonging to the region of Amenti, the abode of the dead ; the others mean belonging to Pharaoh the king. By the same rule we have the names Petamun, Petisis, Petosiris, and others. Line 10 begins with three wavy lines, each an N, and together, the demonstrative sign for water. It ought to begin with one only. This mistake changes the words *priest of* into *libation.* The same mistake is made in line 18. In line 1 we have the same characters without the mistake.

The Two Ends of the Outer Case.

On each end of this case, Plate 3, is a picture between two standing figures of a mummy and four lines of hieroglyphics, with a picture also overhead, in the arched top. In the one head-picture, figure 7, is the character for " good," between two large eyes, figurative of the Divine Providence. Beneath is a priest with shaven head and leopard's skin tunic, in the act of feeding a mummy; and thus reminding us of the command in the Levitical law, which forbad the Jews to give any food to the dead. The inscription under his left hand mentions the thousands of various articles of food. This mummy may be our deceased priest Aroeri thus piously fed ; or the bald-headed priest may be Aroeri, performing this pious act for one of his ancestors. The mummy is held upright by a goddess, probably Isis, who wears on her head the full moon between large cow's horns. It is thus that the new moon is seen when one day old ; the unilluminated part is seen embraced within two horns of light; and in a country like Egypt, near the tropics, these horns are not as with us on one side of the globe, but beneath it. The skin of the priest is red, the colour of the Egyptians, and that of the goddess is blue, to mark her heavenly character.

The inscription contains the often repeated words, (line 5) " The deified priest of Amun, Aroeri, D. S., deceased; (6) son of the priest of Amun Soten-Vaphra, D. S., deceased." Lines 7 and 8 contain exactly the same words repeated.

We might have remarked before that the title given to Aroeri is literally " a man pouring out a libation;" but that given to his father is NOUTE, " divine." The latter we must suppose to be the highest title of the two. We translate them both " priest."

The other head-picture, figure 6, is a sun with rays of light and two sacred asps. On each side is a vase with a flame rising out of it, and then a hawk with a man's head. From this figure the Romans took their notion of a harpy, giving to it however a woman's head instead of a man's, as they did to the sphinx. Beneath is a mummied and bandaged hawk, sitting in a dish, with its name written over it Baal-Sokar. On each side of the hawk, as on the other end, are two standing mummies, and four lines of writing; namely, (line 1) " Honour to the deified priest of Amun, (2) Aroeri, deceased; son of the priest Soten-Vaphra, deceased." Lines 3 and 4 contain the same words repeated.

In lines 2, 4, and 8 the word *son* is written with an egg, in place of the more usual goose.

In line 6 we have the goose. Thus the artist indulged his own taste, and used characters more or less ornamental, according as he wished his work to be handsome and costly or otherwise. In inscriptions made by painting, the characters are usually of a less handsome style than those carved on stone.

The Outside of the Middle Case (Plate 4).

A hole under the chin of the face which ornaments this case tells us that it once had a beard, and represented a man; but the beard has been broken off and lost. The broad black eye-brows and eye-lashes show that it was thought a beauty in men as well as in women to paint that part of the face. What should be the hair of the head, or perhaps a covering for the hair, hangs upon the shoulders, and is painted with alternate stripes of blue and green. The broad collar round the neck is ornamented with several rows of patterns or borders. Amongst others the bell and pomegranate border is three times repeated. It is here formed of round fruit balls and hanging flower bells placed alternately, and all coloured green. But on other Egyptian monuments, and on many Assyrian monuments, it still more closely resembles the border of bells and pomegranates worn by Aaron on the hem of his robe, as described in Exodus xxviii. 34. Other borders on the collar are like rows of leaves placed side by side. One row of leaves is blue and another green.

The two lines of hieroglyphics down the front of this case, figure 8, are in part worn away, but they contain the words "A royal gift dedicated to Osiris Pet-Amenti? great? lord of Thebes. A gift of olive oil, oxen, geese, and various good libations, various * * for the prayer of the deified Aroeri, D. S., deceased; son of the priest of Amun Soten * * * * Onk-Chonso, D. S., deceased; son of [Horus his father Amun] Horseisi, D. S., deceased; son of the priest of Amun Hat * chot, D. S., deceased. His mother the lady of the house Moutresi."

Here the words inclosed within brackets [Horus his father Amun] seem to have been added by the carelessness of the artist. They break the sense, as may be seen by comparing this sentence with several that we have already met on the outer case.

In this inscription the demonstrative sign for a man is a figure seated on a chair, not as before, on the ground. The leg of the chair is copied from the leg of a lion. The man holds in his hand the whip-formed sceptre of Osiris, which tells us that he is dead, and has become an Osiris, or divine person, himself, as indeed we are told by the word Osiris being used as an adjective before his name, which we have translated " deified."

Figures 10 and 11 of Plate 5 are views of the two ends of this middle case. Figure 10 shows the top of the head, with the shoulders, and what may be called the toes. Figure 11 shows the soles of the feet. On the top of the head is the sun, Ra, ornamented with two asps, and followed by his title, " Lord of Ethiopia." The tongue is the word Lord; from the resemblance between ⲗⲁⲥ, a tongue, and ⲥⲓⲥⲓ, lord. So from ⲧⲟⲧ, the hand, we get the sound ⲉⲟⲱϣ, Ethiopia; and the difficulty arising from the want of resemblance is removed by the demonstrative sign for a city, which follows the name.

The sacred asp received its name, Uræus, from the Coptic ⲟⲩⲣⲟ, a king, and its name basilisk, from the Greek βασιλευς, a king. It is the snake called by the naturalists cobra capella. The loose skin upon its head, which gained for it its royal names from its resemblance to a crown, is hardly shown in small drawings. Its better marked feature is its swollen chest, which it causes at pleasure by raising up its ribs. This snake is always used as an emblem of royalty or divinity. It is often the adjective immortal, and is so translated on the Rosetta stone. This is the letter G. A second snake, used as an hieroglyphic, is the small horned snake, the vipera cerastes of the naturalists, which has little fleshy warts on its eyelids, which are here enlarged by the artist into horns. See eight of these in figures 12 and 13. This is the letter F. A third snake in the hieroglyphics is that of which we have also three in figure 12. This probably belongs to the genus *Python*. It is the letter H.

A fourth snake is yet longer than any of these, and used as a letter only in the more modern inscriptions, where we find it as an L in the names of the Roman emperors. But in the sculptures and pictures it is known early and late as the type of sin and wickedness, the enemy of the human race; and in particular in the latter times, as opposed to the Uræus with the swollen chest, which was the type of goodness. From its great length we must suppose that it belongs to the genus *Boa*.

Figure 12 is a side view of this case, showing the arched nose and thick lips of the Egyptian countenance; and also the high ear, which seems however to be a peculiarity arising from a mistaken fashion of the Egyptian artists, rather than from the Egyptian physiognomy. The single line of hieroglyphics which encircles the case must be read from the feet to the head on figure 12, then along the crown of the head on figure 10, and then down the other side of the case again to the feet on figure 13. It is partly the same as the sentences in figure 1, line 15, and figure 4. It may be translated (figure 12), "A royal gift dedicated to Horus-Ra, D.S., chief of the heavenly gods; Chem, lord of the land of San; Pthah-Sokar-Osiris, god, lord of * * *; Anubis, chief of the temple; a gift of things dedicated, things sacred, other good libations * * * * for the prayers of the deified priest of (figure 10) Amun, Aroeri, deceased; son of the priest (figure 13) of Amun, Soten-Vaphra, D.S., deceased; son of the priest Onk-Chonso, deceased. His mother is the lady of the house Hatresi, deceased * * * Osiris, lord of the region of Amenti, god, chief of * * * * * * Amenti, good * * lord of * * city, Osiris."

There is only this one line of painting on the side of the outside of the middle case, and none on the back; and, as there is no painting on the inside of the outer case, we must suppose that these two were not meant to be parted. Hence also we see that the mummy cases were meant to be opened from time to time. The painting was not made to be put away and never looked at, but was so arranged that if the lid of the outer case were lifted off, and then the lid of the middle case lifted off, and then the inner case wholly lifted out, and opened, and examined all round, inside and out, no want of ornament would be seen while the back half of the middle case remained in its place.

The Inside of the Middle Case.

On the inside of the back half of the middle case, figure 9, Plate 4, is painted one of the four lesser gods of the dead. It is a human figure the size of life, bandaged like a mummy, and standing in profile, with a hawk's head, like Horus. The blue colour of his hands, the only flesh that is seen, declares his spiritual nature. On his head is the tall conical crown of Upper Egypt, with a ball at the top, and two feathers beside it as wings. In front of it is the sacred asp, the usual ornament of a king's forehead. His two hands hold an Anubis-staff, the dog-headed staff which was often carried by the priests. This was the staff which the emperor Commodus was ambitious of being allowed to carry in the procession of Isis, in Rome; and he had his head shaved like a priest, to qualify him for the office. See Lampridius, *Vita Commodi*.

By the side of this god is written his name Smotef, *the carver*, who usually has a jackall's head, and is sometimes also named Sottef, a word with nearly the same meaning.

The Outside of the Inner Case (Plates 6 and 7).

The inner case is the most handsome of the three, the most carefully painted inside and out, and perhaps by a better artist than the painter of the cases already described; it is also better preserved. The face which, in the middle case, was of a dark acacia wood, approaching to ebony in its colour, is here painted red, of a colour not far removed from that of the Egyptians themselves. The beard is a thin piece of wood fixed into the chin, painted to imitate plaited hair, and straight, except that the end is slightly curled forward, a peculiarity which we remark upon the stone mummy cases in the British Museum, of the three or four centuries before the Christian era. All hair is shaven off the cheek, in which respects the face is unlike those of the Theban kings, where the painted whisker on the cheek looks almost like a band by which the beard is held on. But in a priest like Aroeri-ao, we remark with surprise, not that the beard at the point of the chin is the only hair on his face, but that he wears any beard at all. What should be the hair of the head is of alternate stripes of blue and yellow. On the breast is the figure of the goddess Neith, sitting with outstretched arms. Corresponding with her is the figure of the goddess Isis, upon the instep, in the same attitude. When the two goddesses are so opposed, Neith represents power over heavenly things, and Isis over earthly things.

The hieroglyphics and pictures of the front, in figure 14, must be first described. The single line of hieroglyphics running down the front, and the six lines running across, divide the front into ten squares. In the top row are the four lesser gods of the dead; viz., Amset *the carpenter*, with a man's head; Hepe *the digger*, with an ape's head; Smotef *the cutter*, with a hawk's head; and Snouf *the bleeder*, with a jackal's head. In the second row are two gods with jackals' heads, each named Anubis. In the third row are the hawk-headed Horus and the ibis-headed Thoth, with a hippopotamus-headed god behind each, and behind these, Isis on one side and her sister Nephthys on the other side. In the fourth row are two hawks with large outstretched wings, and suns on their heads. In front of each is the eye, Baal, for its name. In the fifth row is Seb and Ra.

On each shoulder is a line of hieroglyphics with the name and parentage of the deceased, who is here called Arocri-ao, and his father is said to be " deceased, immortal," thus marking in the very language the belief in a future life. Here the word ⲚⲞⲧⲧⲉ, *god* or *priest*, is spelt with a final vowel, as it is again in line 4, and as is the name Soten-Vaphra in line 2. This is an exactness not often met with in hieroglyphics.

Line 1 is in honour of the goddess Neith, and it contains the word "mummy," spelt MM, and followed by the demonstrative sign of a hawk sitting on a lion-formed couch, the couch on which the mummy was usually laid.

Line 5 contains the name " Soten-Vaphra," spelt not with a rabbit for the syllable SOT, but with a star-shaped flower, which has the same sound. It is by the comparison of words, when thus spelt in two ways, that we learn the force of characters otherwise new to us.

Line 6 is in honour of the goddess Isis, whose figure is on the instep.

On the back of this case, figure 15, is painted a nilometer-landmark, girded with a sash, and having on the top the ornaments which belong to the head of a god; namely, the rams horns of Kneph, with the sun and ostrich feathers of Amun-ra, further ornamented with two asps, one wearing the crown of Upper Egypt and the other of Lower. This landmark or boundary-stone is named ⲦⲀⳓ, *a boundary*; and its name is proved by its being met with in its doubled form in the Rosetta stone, as ⲦⲀⳓⲦⲀⳓ, *established*. And further, from the connection in the Egyptian mind between writing and the pillar on which it was written, this boundary-stone, the *deus Terminus* of the Romans, became Thoth, the god of writing.

The two crowns worn by the serpents on the top of this column are the mitre and crown worn by the Jewish high priests. The mitre has a ball on the top, and is the crown of Upper Egypt. The crown is a plate of metal with no top to it, and is the crown of Lower Egypt. When the mitre is placed upon the head, and then the crown placed over the mitre, as directed in Exodus xxix. 6, the two form the double crown called the Pschent in the Rosetta decree. This double crown is seen upon the steersman of the boat of Ra, in figure 1, Plate 1.

By the side of this landmark are sixty-five short lines of hieroglyphics, containing many sentences the same as those on the outer cases. The other sentences are not so easily understood. We remark, however, in lines 15, 16, Aroeri-ao is called " deceased, illustrious," and the latter word is that translated Epiphanes, as the title of Ptolemy V. in the Rosetta decree. In line 48 we read " deep waters ;" of which the former word is spelt HBB, from ℨⲃⲃⲉ, *deep*. In lines 51, 52, we read, " the appointed door-keeper of the two doors of heaven," a title not uncommon in the inscriptions.

In line 26 is mentioned the god Aten-Ra, whose name seems formed from the Hebrew word Adonai, *lord*, a name found in the inscriptions both early and late, but particularly during the reigns of the Persians. The name of the Egyptian who rebelled against Artaxerxes was by the Greeks written Inarus, but his true name seems to have been Aten-ra Bakan. In line 28 is mentioned the god Seb, the father of the gods.

Figure 16 is a side view of this inner case which we have been describing.

Figure 17 shows the painting at the bottom of its feet, where the bull Apis, with a golden asp between its horns, is carrying this very mummy case, which lies upon its back.

Figure 18, by the painting on the top of the head, seems to show that the priest Aroeri-ao did not shave his head wholly bald, but left his hair at the back, while the fore part of the top was neatly shaven like the Roman Catholic tonsure. This custom the Christian clergy copied from the Egyptian priests. On the bald part of the head is painted a scarabæus, or beetle, with its hind legs upon a ring, which is probably an R, as the mouth is often so placed. The scarabæus is HO, and, with the ring, HOR, or Horus. It holds between its front legs a ball of dirt in which the insect lays its eggs. This is the sun, Ra ; and together they form the word, and represent the god Horus-Ra, after whom the deceased was named, and who may be called his patron saint.

The Inside of the Inner Case (Plate 8).

The inside of this case is the most ornamented part of the whole. It has one large figure painted on the upper half or front, and one on the lower half or back.

On the back half, figure 19, is the Thoth, or nilometer-landmark before described, with the same girdle and crown, but here having a human head and arms. The flesh is painted blue, to mark that it is the figure of a god. In his hands he holds the two sceptres which are peculiar to Osiris, one a whip, and one a crook. This figure therefore is at the same time Thoth and Osiris and Kneph-Ra. Over his head is written " Ra, the great god, lord of Ethiopia." The tongue is *lord*; the hand, ⲧⲟⲧ, stands for ⲉⲟⲱⲩⲏ, *Ethiopia*. This hand, when the position is changed, is the Hebrew letter ⲧ; and we remark that the Hebrews, in borrowing the letter from Egypt, took with it its Egyptian name Teth.

On the right side of this figure, beginning at his head, is written, " Glory dedicated to Chem, for the Egyptian priests of the temple. Appointed door-keeper of heaven, appointed for earth, appointed door-keeper for the city, appointed door-keeper of holy Amenti, for the deified priest of Amun, Aroeri-ao, a man deceased, full of blessings." " Chem" is here spelt with a final M, which is wanted in the inscription on the outer case. " Egyptians" is spelt Chemo, such being the usual plural termination.

On the left side of the figure is a line of writing, beginning with the parentage of the deceased; but then changing, as follows : " I am Tosh-tosh of Ethiopia, son of Tosh," which, as we have before conjectured, is another name for Thoth. This figure stands upon the representation of a house, with a door; and the characters upon it perhaps describe it as the temple of the bull Apis.

On the upper half of this case, figure 20, is the goddess Neith, with her arms outstretched, to receive the deceased priest. Her name is written within the circle on her head, spelt NT, and followed by the figure of the heavens as the demonstrative sign. Her face, arms, and feet are yellow, the colour always given to the Egyptian women, marking that their skin is fairer than that of the men. Her hair is blue, as is the greater part of her dress; but her body is not of the human form, it is nothing but an enlarged sash-tye. Around her head is written " Mother of the glorious gods." Under her left elbow is " Her gift, her glory," where the letter S is the feminine pronoun *her*, as the letter F is usually the masculine *his*. Over her feet is written " mummy," followed by the mummy-couch as the demonstrative sign. The sentence on her right side, beginning at her wrist, begins, " Loftiness is thy name for ever;" spelt Ϭⲓⲥⲓ, *loftiness*, ⲣⲁⲛ, *name*, ⲕ, *thy*. The sentence on her left seems to end with " her name is door;" spelt ⲣⲁⲛ, *name*, ⲥ, *her*, ⲡⲉⲛⲛⲉ, *door*; a reading which seems not improbable after the title of " door-keeper to heaven," which we have before met with.

Over her head we read " Ra, the great god, lord of Ethiopia;" and he is also styled Oben-Ra, a name which seems only an Asiatic way of pronouncing Amun-Ra, and which may have been brought into Egypt by the Persians. We find the same name written in hieroglyphics on an ivory box in the British Museum, which was brought from Nineveh.

The gods named in the inscriptions are not few in number. They are, 1, Horus-Ra, the chief of the gods; 2, Horus the son of Isis; 3, Isis; 4, Nephthys her sister; 5, Osiris, ruler of Amenti; 6, the Sokar god; 7, Pthah-Sokar-Osiris of Memphis; 8 and 9, two of the name of Anubis; 10, Amun; 11, Chem, lord of San or Tanis; 12, Seb; 13, Neith, the mother of the gods, who belonged to Sais; the four lesser gods of the dead, namely, 14, Smotef; 15, Amset; 16, Hepi; 17, Snouf; 18, Oben-Ra; 19, Aten-Ra; 20, Chonso. Thus we have no mention of Amun-Ra of Thebes, nor of Athor his wife, nor of Chonso their son, except as part of a man's name; nor of Pasht the goddess of Bubastis; nor of Apis-Osiris, better known as Serapis; nor of Hapimou the Nile.

Throughout the whole of the long inscriptions there is no date, either of time or place; indeed the mummy cases seldom have a king's name upon them to guide us. We must form our opinion of the date from the style of art and any peculiarities that the inscription affords. From these it seems probable that our mummy was made in Memphis, during the reigns of the Persian conquerors of Egypt, or about four hundred years before the Christian era. The absence of the Theban gods from the list shows that it belonged to Lower Egypt; the absence of Serapis, and of all Greek peculiarities, marks it older than the Ptolemies. The name of Oben-Ra, which we also find on the sarcophagus of Amyrtæus (see *Egyptian Inscriptions*, Plate 30), leads us to the same century. The box-like form of the outer case, the sash-tye which forms the body of the goddess in Plate 8, both belong rather to Memphis than to Thebes.

The mummy and inner mummy case of Horseisi, the great grandfather of Aroeri-ao, are in the museum of the College of Surgeons, ornamented with paintings, in a style not unlike those of his great grandson.

E

As we have remarked upon the Egyptian origin of the Hebrew and Greek alphabets, we here add the hieroglyphics from which they seem to have been derived, as also those which were the originals of the six Coptic letters, which were in the second century added to the Greek alphabet, to form the Coptic alphabet for the Christians.

Hebrew Letters.   Greek Letters.

a
p
g
d t
e
f
z
th t
i
k
l r
m
n
sh s
n
s sh

a
п
г
Δ
є
F
ζ
H
Θ
I
K
Λ

M
N
O
P
Σ
C
σ
T
Υ
Φ
X
Ψ

Six hieroglyphics with the new Coptic letters formed from them.

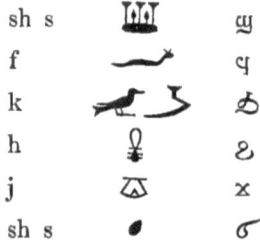

sh s
f
k
h
j
sh s

For those Hebrew and Greek letters which are formed by varying others in the same alphabet, of course we have no originals in hieroglyphics. And it may be further remarked, the Hebrew letters Teth, Nun, and Pe took from Egypt not only their form but their names, which mean in Coptic, *hand, water,* and *the heavens.* It will be observed that many of the letters which lie down in the hieroglyphics are made to stand up in the Greek and Hebrew alphabets.

Fig 2

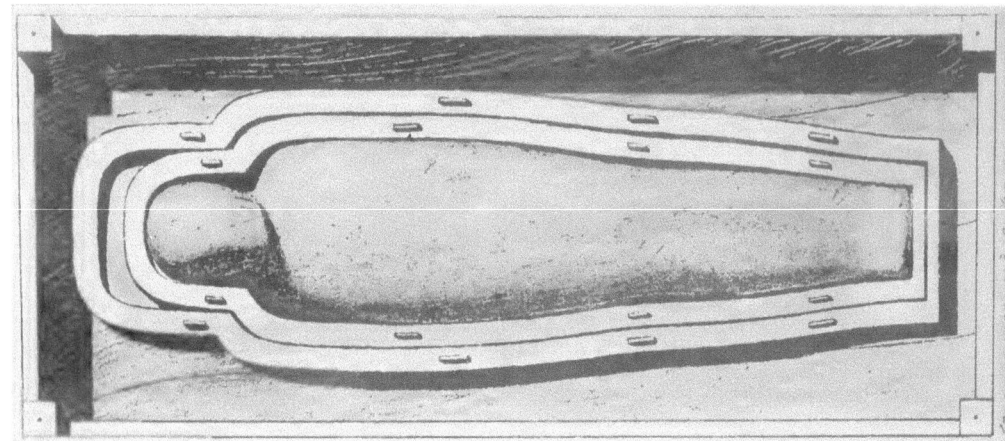

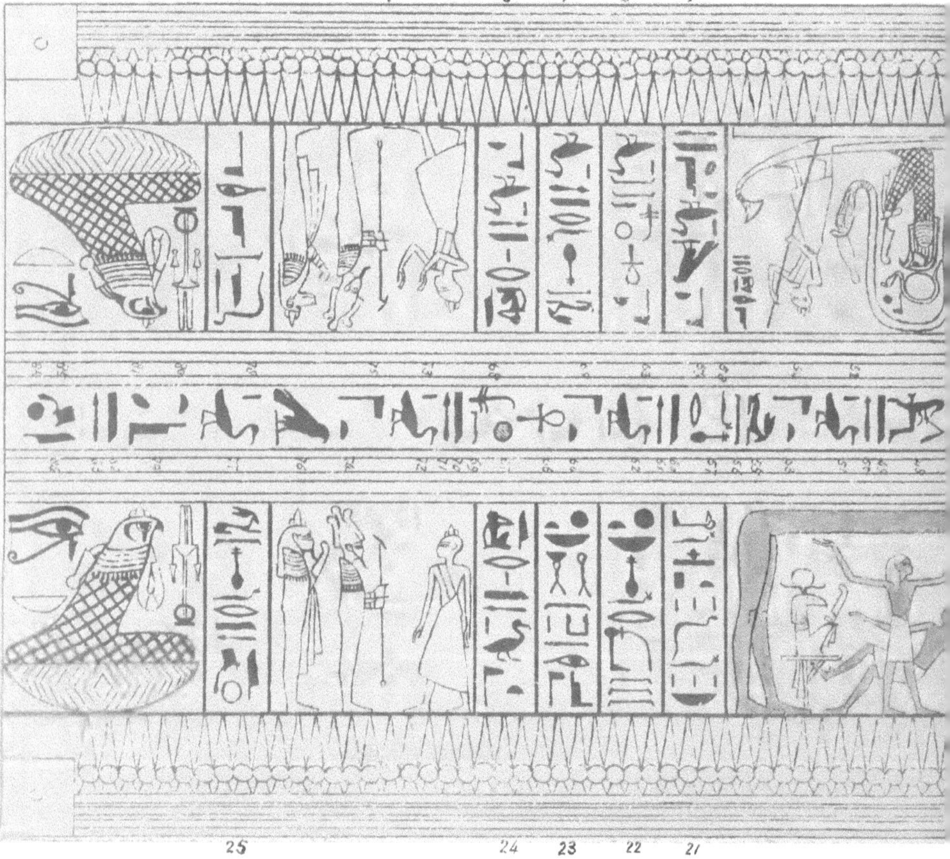

PLATE 1

Fig. 3

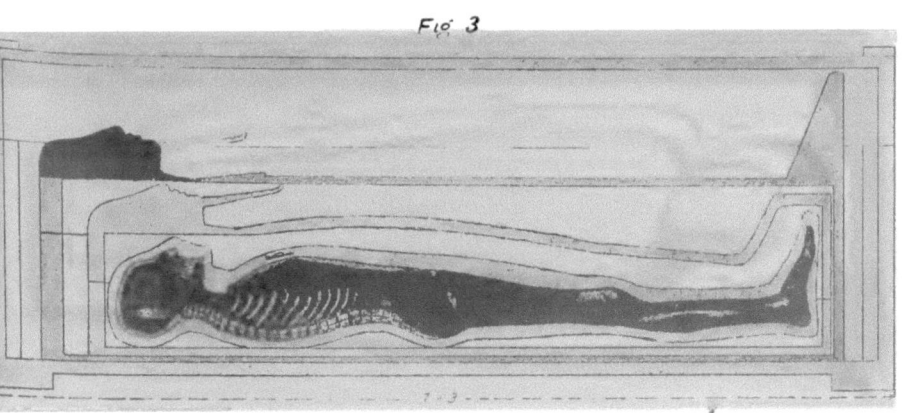

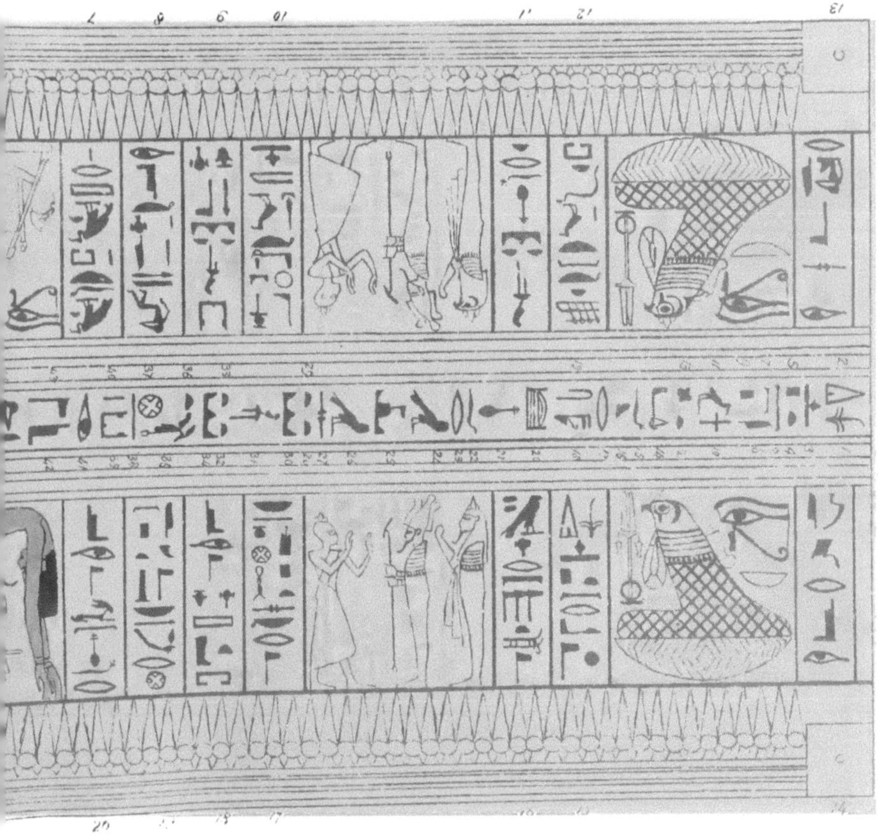

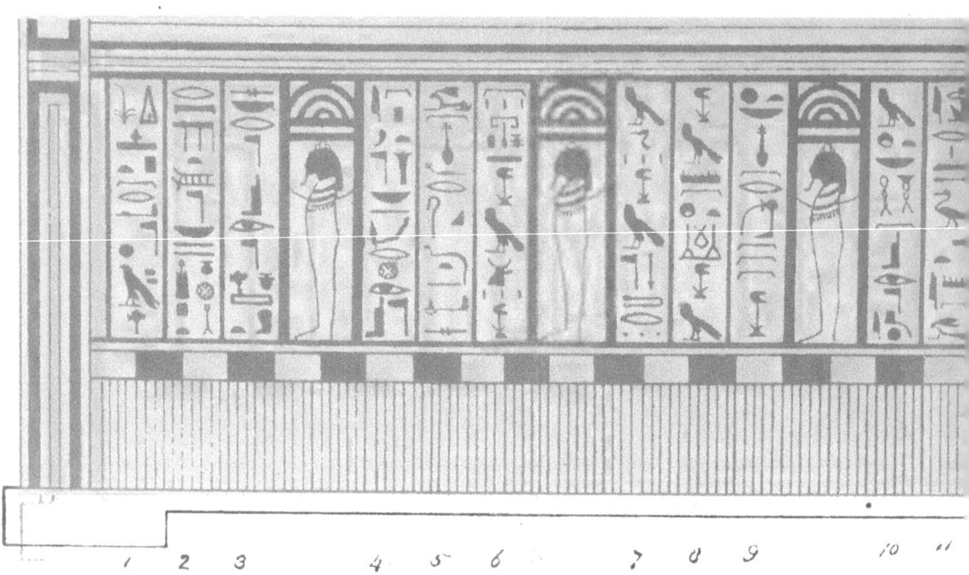
1 2 3 4 5 6 7 8 9 10 11

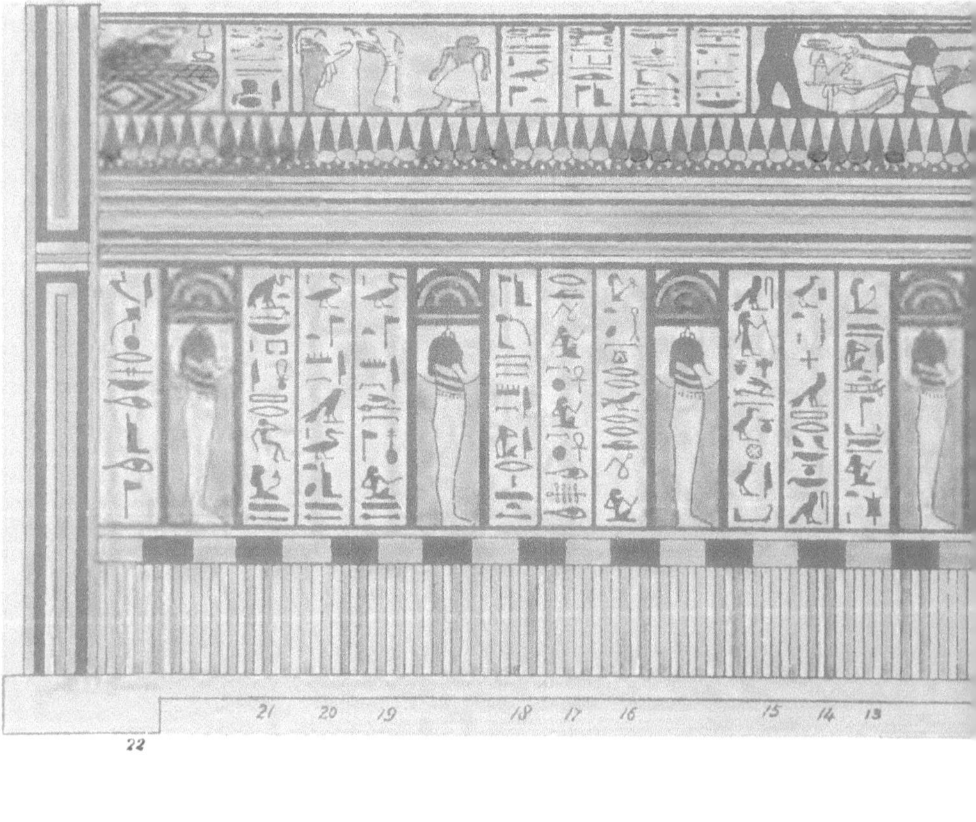
21 20 19 18 17 16 15 14 13
22

PLATE 2

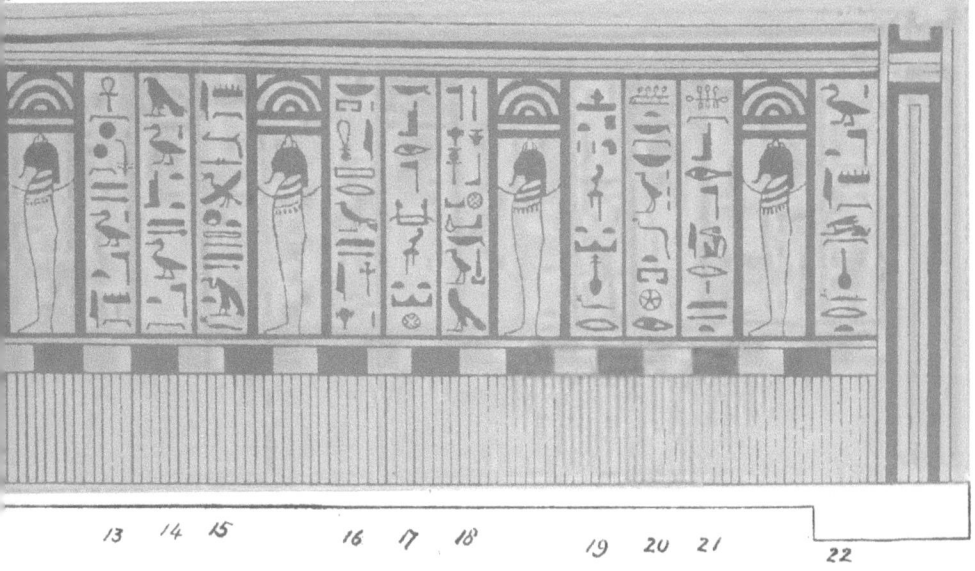

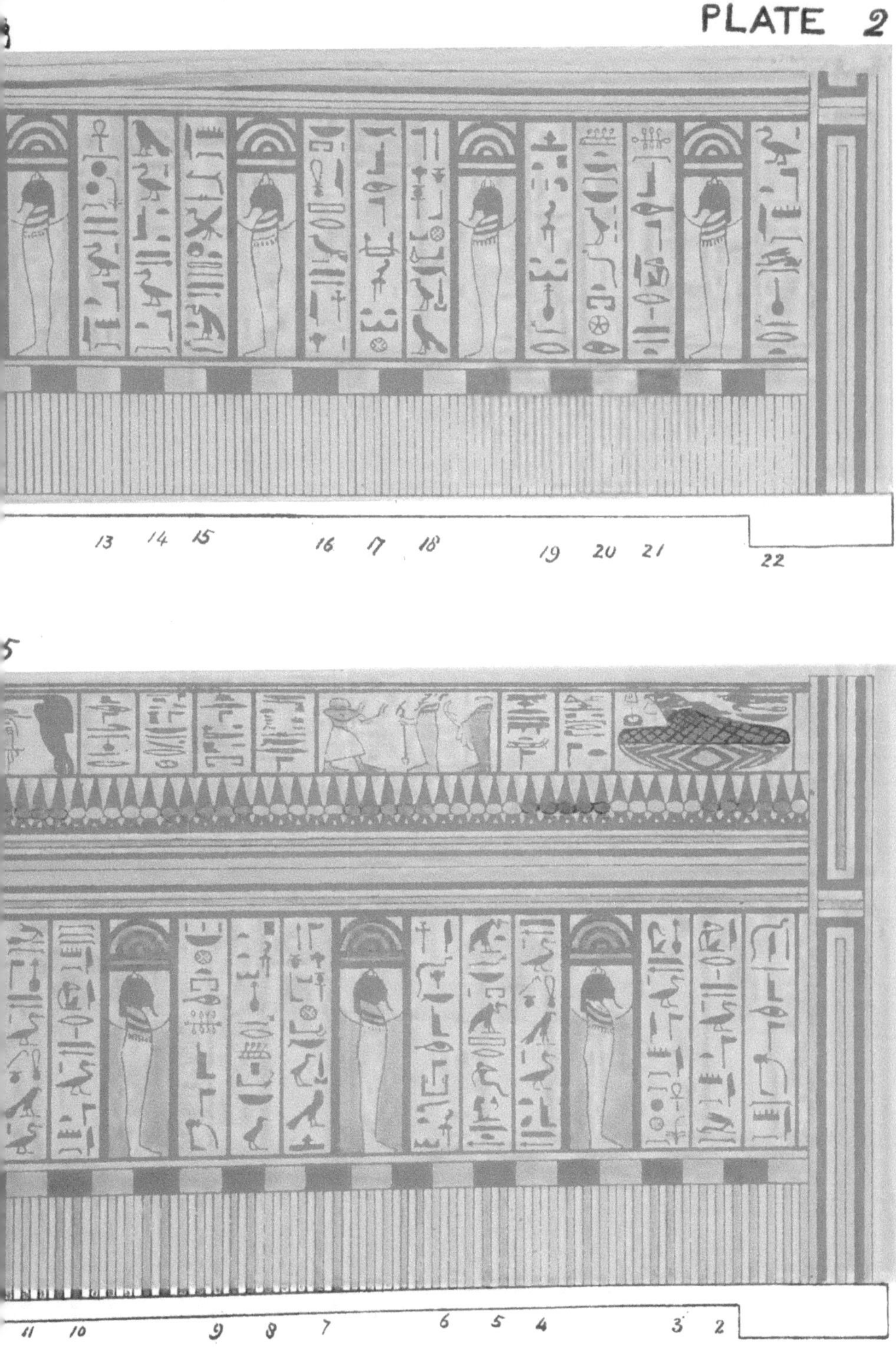

13 14 15   16 17 18   19 20 21   22

11 10   9 8 7   6 5 4   3 2

Bonomi Del

Fig. 6

2   1   3   4

PLATE 3

Fig 7

Fig. 8

Fig. 9

PLATE 4

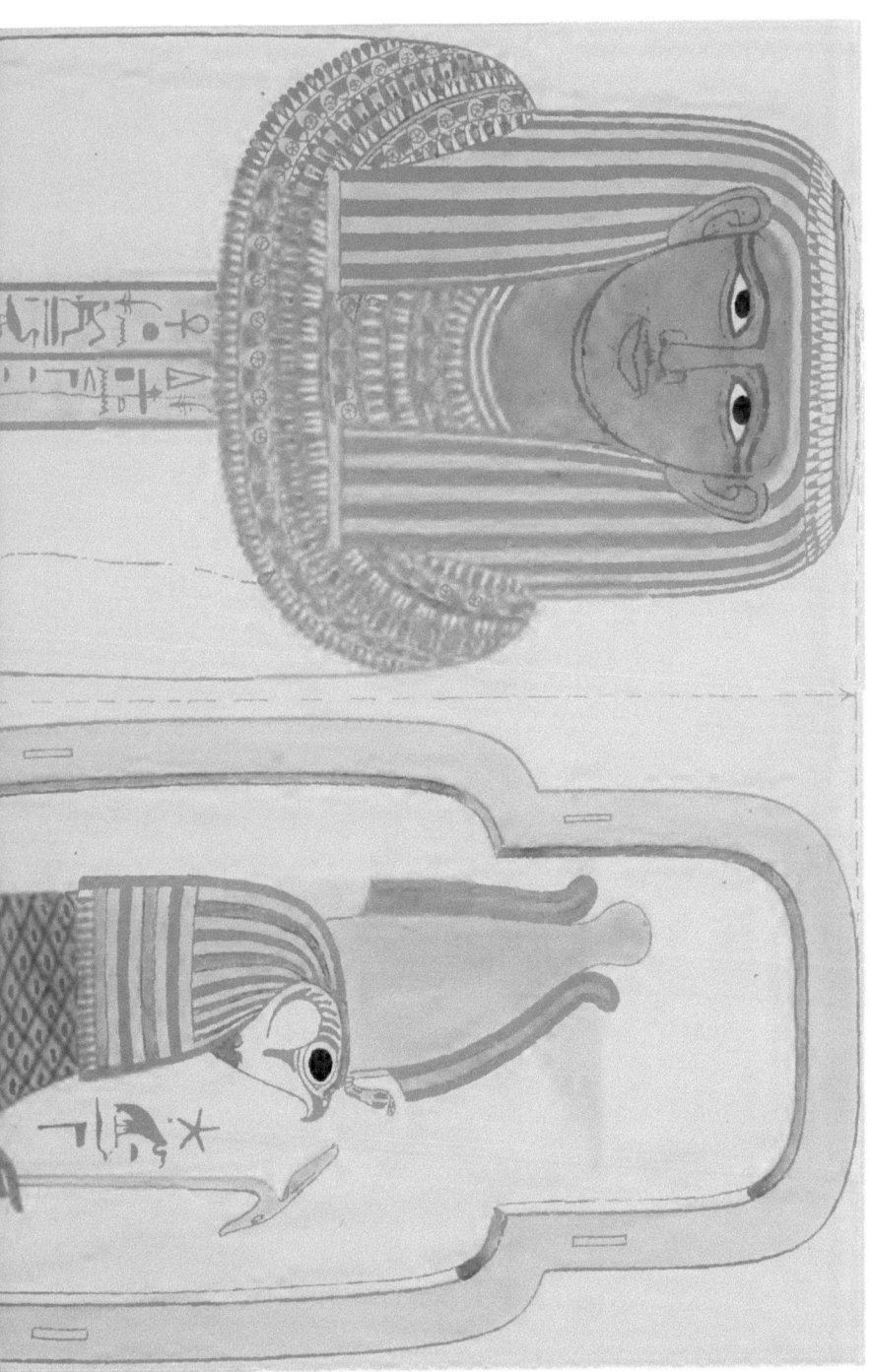

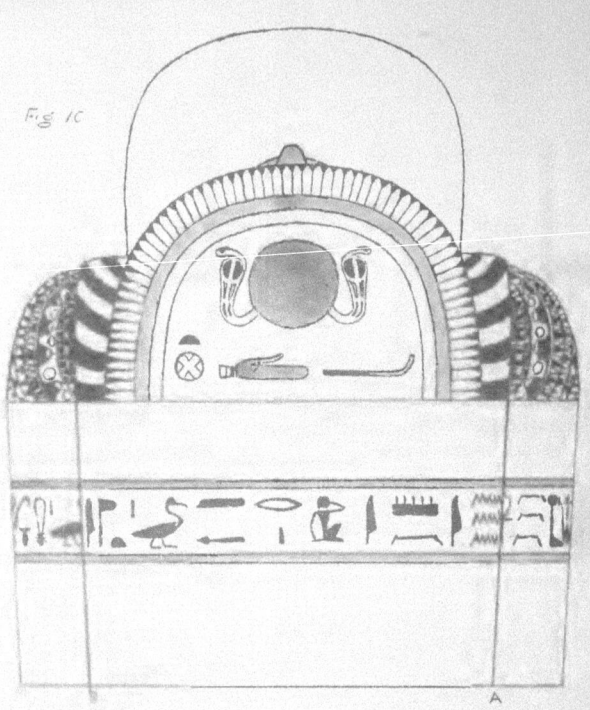

Fig 1C

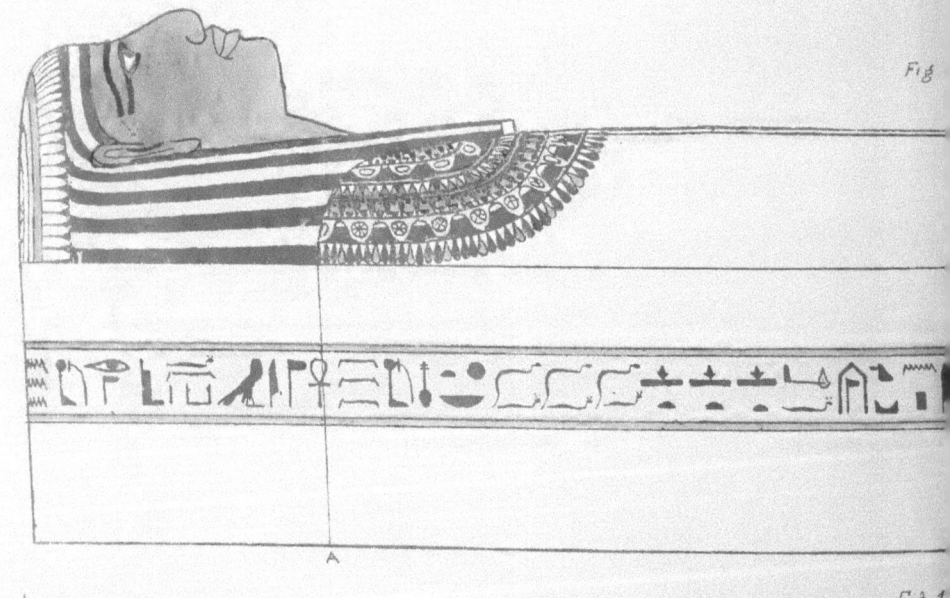

Fig

A

Fig 1

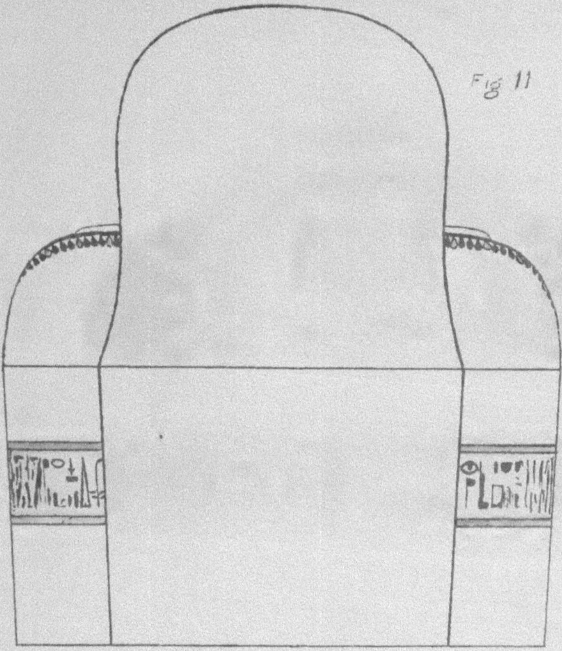

PLATE 5

Fig 11

2

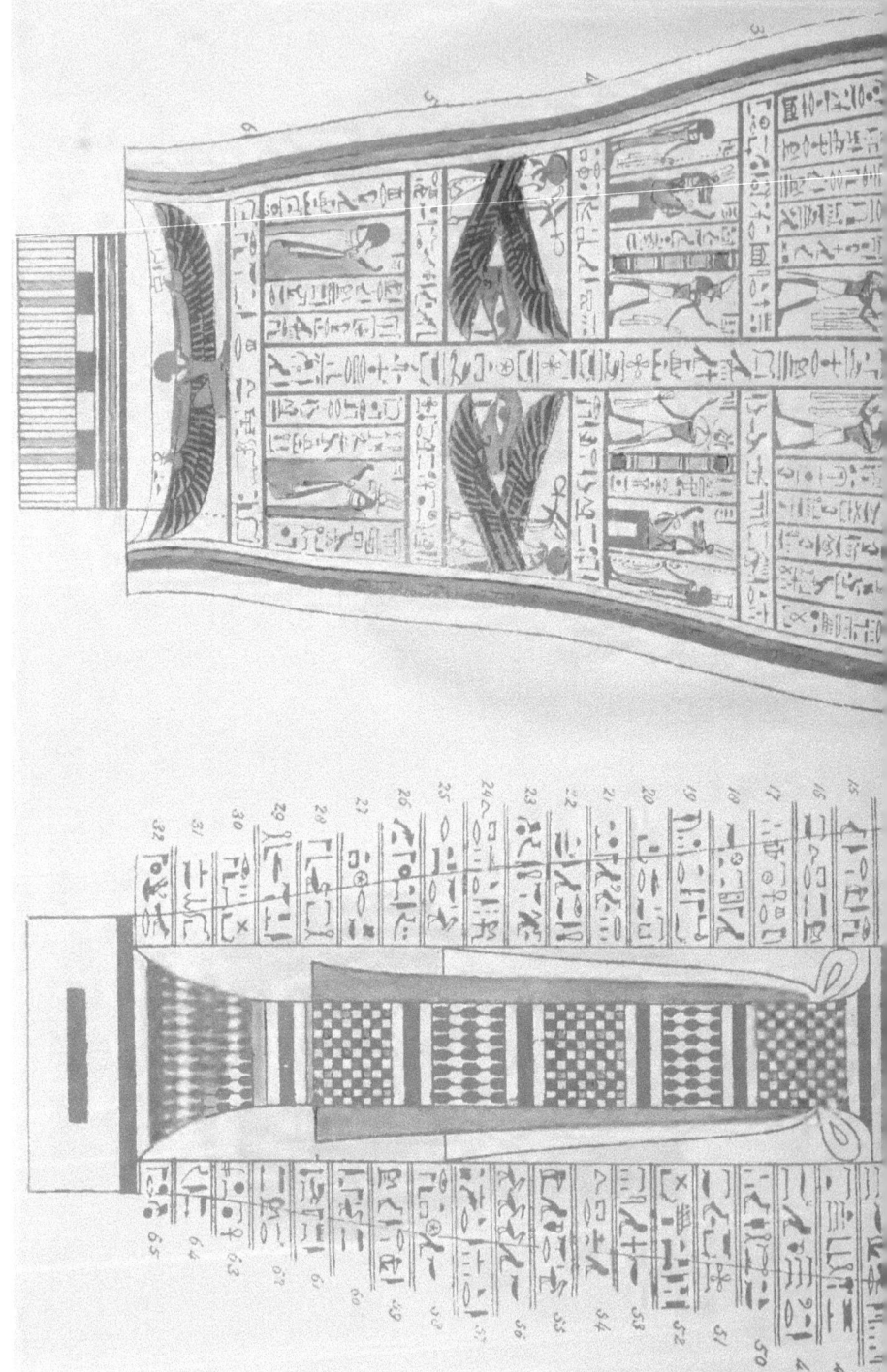

Bonomi Del

PLATE 6

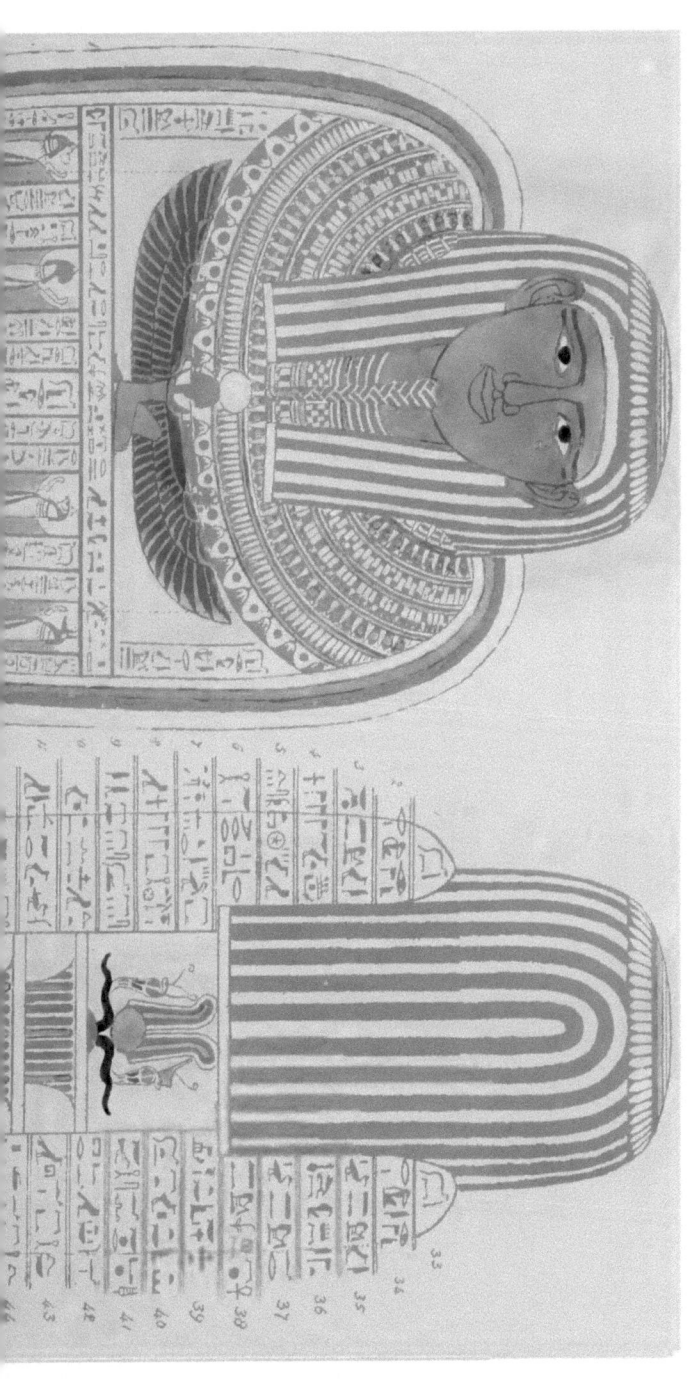

Fig 14

Fig 15

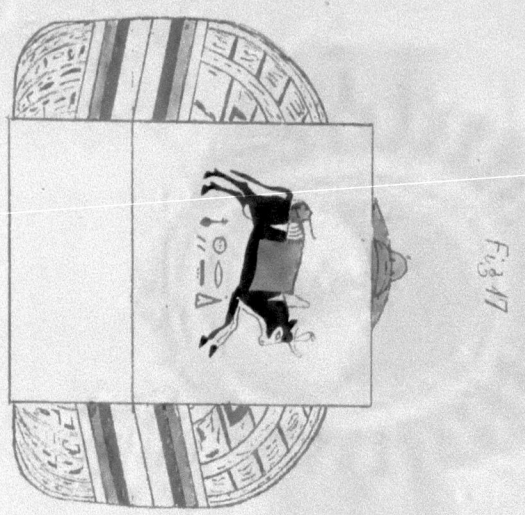

Fig. 17

PLATE 7

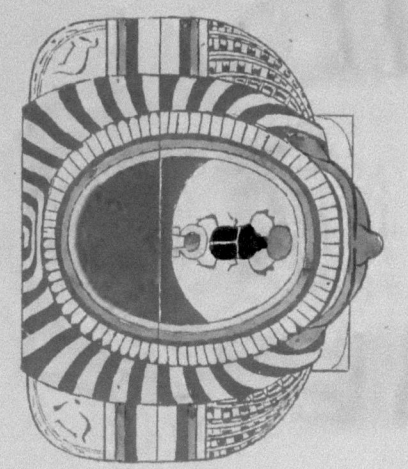

Fig 18

Fig 16

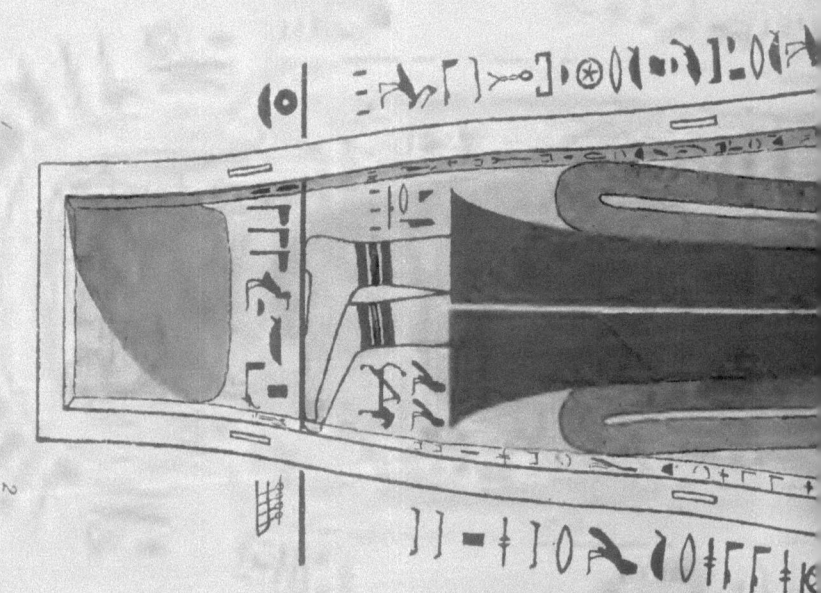

BONOMI DEL.

PLATE 8

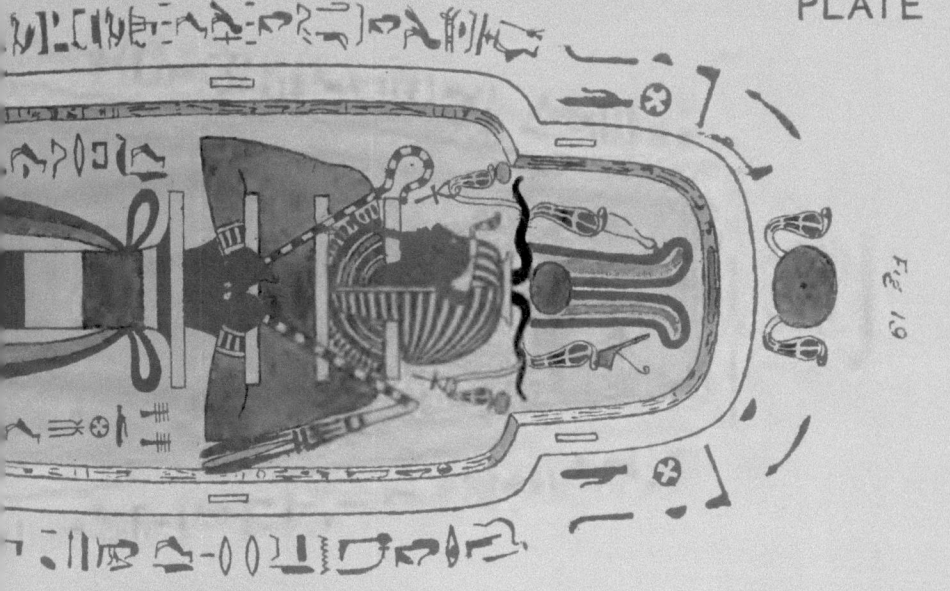

Fig 19

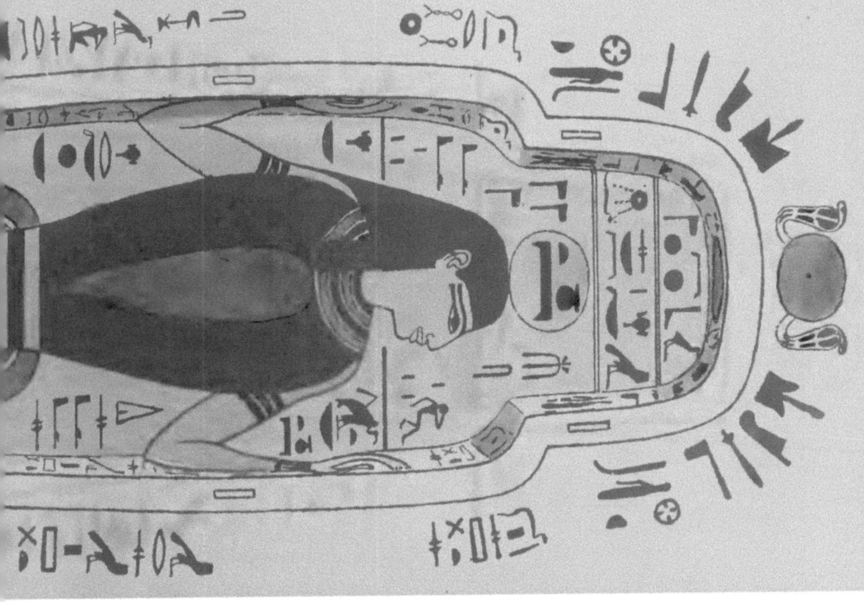

Fig 20